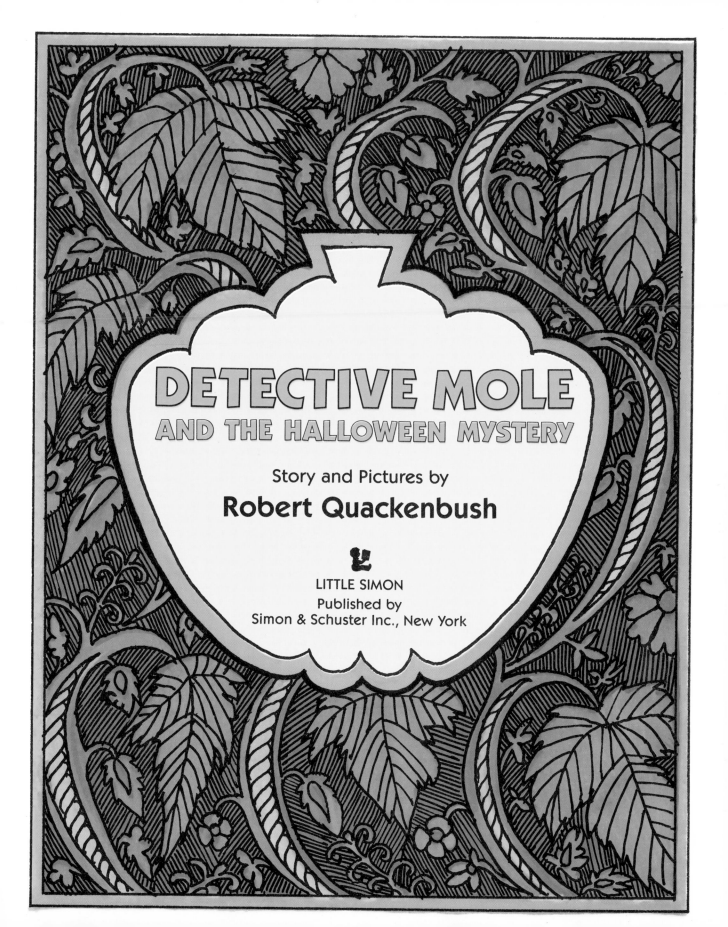

DETECTIVE MOLE
AND THE HALLOWEEN MYSTERY

Story and Pictures by

Robert Quackenbush

LITTLE SIMON
Published by
Simon & Schuster Inc., New York

Little Simon
Simon & Schuster Building
Rockefeller Center
1230 Avenue of the Americas
New York, New York 10020

Copyright © 1981 by Robert Quackenbush

All rights reserved
including the right of reproduction
in whole or in part in any form.

LITTLE SIMON and colophon are trademarks
of Simon & Schuster Inc.

Manufactured in the United States of America

10   9   8   7   6   5   4   3

ISBN 0-671-67830-2

The town was in an uproar. Nothing like it had happened before. Every jack-o'-lantern had been stolen from every front porch. And that very night was Halloween!

Detective Mole's phone rang all day. Armed with a magnifying glass and a pocketful of jellybeans to snack on, he ran from house to house searching for clues.

At last, a break came in the case when Detective Mole investigated the robbery of the Chicken family's jack-o'-lantern. He found a pair of big, fancy glasses, shaped like cat's eyes, under the porch of the chicken coop. The lenses were thick and very strong.

"Hmmm," he said. "Mrs. Cat wears glasses."

"Surely you don't suspect Mrs. Cat?" cried Mrs. Hen. "She would never commit a robbery. Besides, her jack-o'-lantern was stolen, too."

Detective Mole replied, "Mrs. Hen, everyone is a suspect in this case, even our best friends. I'll have to check this out."

He walked over to Mr. and Mrs. Cat's house. He asked Mrs. Cat to try on the glasses and walk across the room.

"Ohh…" she said, "they make my head spin." Then she tried to take a step and fell flat on the floor.

"Sorry about that," said Detective Mole, as he and Mr. Cat helped Mrs. Cat up from the floor. "But thank you for your cooperation. You have proved that the glasses are not for your eyes."

Mr. Cat said, "Maybe the glasses are a trick to throw off suspicion from the real crook."

"That's possible," said Detective Mole. "We would know if they are fake if we knew the motive for the crime. The motive would give us a clearer picture of the thief."

"Maybe someone wants the jack-o'-lanterns for a giant pumpkin pie," said Mrs. Cat.

"Hmmm," said Detective Mole. "But who in this town has that big an appetite?"

Mr. and Mrs. Cat looked at each other and gasped.

"ELMO ELEPHANT!" they cried.

Detective Mole shuddered. Elmo was everybody's friend. Still, he was duty-bound to overlook no one as a suspect, not even Elmo.

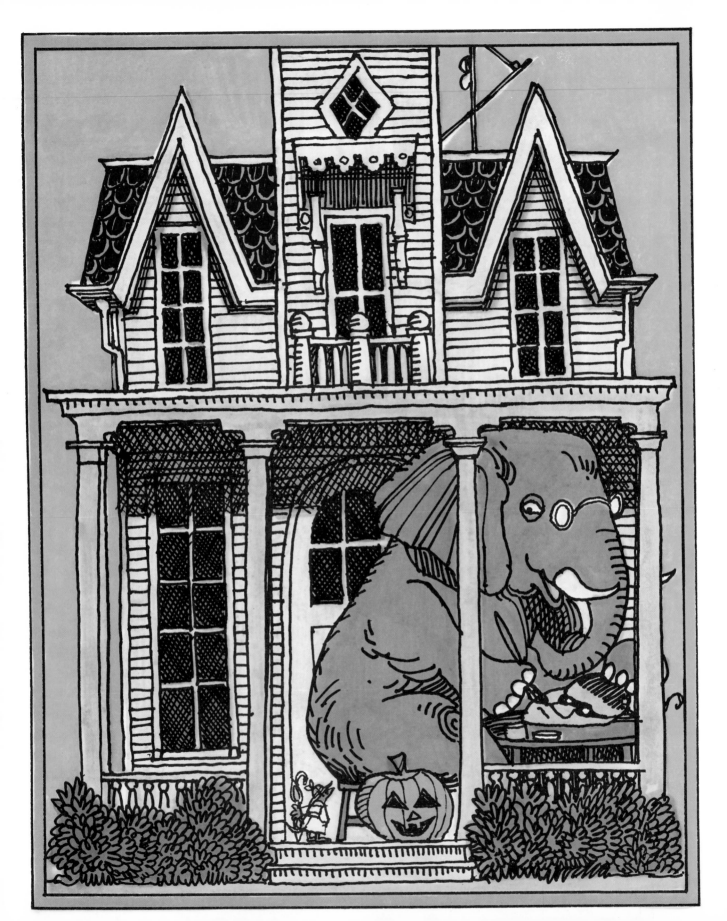

Detective Mole went to Elmo's house. Elmo was sitting on his porch making a mask for Halloween. Right in plain sight at his feet was a jack-o'-lantern!

After a friendly exchange of greetings, Detective Mole said, "I must ask you something, Elmo. How is it that you have a jack-o'-lantern, when no one else has one?"

"Oh," said Elmo. "That's because I just finished carving the face."

Detective Mole had to be sure that Elmo was telling the truth. He looked at the jack-o'-lantern with his magnifying glass. Sure enough, the cut marks in the pumpkin were still fresh.

"Tell me, Elmo," Detective Mole asked quickly. "Do you like pumpkin pie?"

"No," answered Elmo. "But if *you* do, you are welcome to my pumpkin after Halloween."

Detective Mole heaved a sigh of relief. Now he knew that everybody's friend, Elmo, was in the clear. He thanked Elmo for his offer of the pumpkin and reached in his pocket for a handful of jellybeans.

"Join me?" asked Detective Mole.

"Glad to," replied Elmo.

While the two were munching jellybeans, Detective Mole kept eyeing Elmo's jack-o'-lantern. He was sure the thief would want to steal it. Then he thought of a way to catch the thief. He whispered the plan to Elmo.

The plan was to have Elmo leave the house so it would appear deserted, but Detective Mole would be hiding in the jack-o'-lantern. Then, when the thief came, Detective Mole would leap out and capture the culprit.

"But what if there are a number of thieves?" asked Elmo.

"Then I'll make a run for it," said Detective Mole, "and seek help."

Everything was decided. Elmo pretended he was going shopping. As he walked down the road, Detective Mole climbed into the jack-o'-lantern and waited for the thief.

It was damp inside the jack-o'-lantern and the odor of fresh pumpkin was very strong. It made Detective Mole's head very heavy. He wished the thief would hurry and get there.

Detective Mole's head got heavier and heavier. He fell fast asleep.

Detective Mole woke up with a start. He was being tossed about inside the jack-o'-lantern. Too late! While he was asleep, someone had grabbed the jack-o'-lantern and was running away with it.

Detective Mole held on tight to the wall of the jack-o'-lantern. He looked out the openings. He could see a full harvest moon rising, but he couldn't see the thief. He wondered where he was being taken. How would anyone be able to find him?

He reached for a jellybean to take his mind off his worries. "I've got it!" he thought.

He began tossing jellybeans out of the jack-o'-lantern's grinning mouth. The candy fell to the ground and made a shiny trail in the moonlight.

At last, Detective Mole could see where he was being taken. Just ahead was the old, abandoned house that folks in town had been saying was haunted. For about a year, lights had been going on and off in the windows. And *always* very late at night.

"So that's it!" thought Detective Mole. "Someone very much alive, not a ghost, has been haunting that old house. It's been a hideout for the thief. But who is the thief? I've ruled out everyone in town."

Detective Mole hung on for dear life as he and the jack-o'-lantern were carried up the steps of the old house and through the front door. Then the jack-o'-lantern was placed on the floor. Detective Mole saw that he was in a room filled with the town's stolen jack-o'-lanterns!

A door slammed. All was quiet. When Detective Mole was
sure it was safe, he climbed out of Elmo's jack-o'-lantern.

"Now!" he thought. "It's time to have a look at the thief!"

He crept across the room and opened the door very
slowly. He saw some steps going down to a cellar. At the
bottom of the steps he saw someone he had never seen before.
He saw a black cat wearing a tall pointed hat. The cat was
busy packing some things in a small bundle. The cat looked
up for a moment, but didn't see Detective Mole.

"Well, I'll be!" thought Detective Mole. "A witch!"

There wasn't a moment to waste. Everyone had to be told about the thief so that they could get their jack-o'-lanterns back in time for Halloween.

He closed the cellar door quietly and raced from room to room until he found the front door of the house. He pulled it open and froze in his tracks. There, looming in front of him, stood Frankenstein's monster!

"Elmo!" cried Detective Mole. "What a fright you gave me. How did you know to come here?"

"It was quite simple," said Elmo. "I went back home to see if you were safe. When I saw my jack-o'-lantern was gone, I knew your plan had worked. Then I saw your jelly-bean trail and guessed that you might be in trouble. I grabbed my Halloween mask and followed it."

"And just in time, too, Elmo," said Detective Mole. "Please listen to me carefully and do as I say. I have no time to explain. I'll close the door and when it opens again, in a few minutes, yell 'trick or treat' as loud as you can."

Detective Mole closed the front door. Then he ran to the cellar door and opened it wide.

"Yoo hoo, Witch!" he shouted down the cellar steps. "Catch me if you can!"

The cat tore up the steps and chased Detective Mole through the house. They came to the front door. Quickly, Detective Mole pulled the door open.

"TRICK OR TREAT!" roared Elmo.

"*Yeeoooo!*" screeched the cat. In a flash, it leaped up and grabbed a ceiling light fixture.

"We've caught you red-handed, Witch," said Detective Mole. "Come down and tell us why you stole our jack-o'-lanterns."

"Ohhhh!" cried the cat. "Where *are* my glasses? All I can see is a big, blurry shape!"

"Aha!" said Detective Mole. "Don't worry. That's only my friend Elmo Elephant in costume. Come on down, Witch."

"Stop calling me 'Witch'!" cried the cat. "I am not a witch. I am a witch's cat. My name is Sheba. And I didn't do anything wrong."

"Sorry, Sheba," said Detective Mole, "but your glasses are just the proof I need."

Detective Mole got the glasses from Elmo's jack-o'-lantern. He showed them to Sheba.

"Give them to me!" cried Sheba. "I need them!"

"I'll give them to you when you come down," said Detective Mole. "But you must tell us everything."

Sheba sat on the light fixture and glared at Detective Mole. Finally, she gave in and jumped down from the fixture. She retrieved her glasses and put them on.

"Okay, I'll talk," she said. "It all began last year at Halloween. That's when my mistress, who is a very important witch, lost me."

"A witch? You mean the human kind?" asked Detective Mole.

Sheba nodded and went on, "We were flying over your town when I accidentally fell off the broom. My mistress is even more nearsighted than I am and it was very dark. I heard her flying overhead trying to find me. Finally, she had to go on her way without me because they can't start the Halloween Witches' Council without her. I have been hiding here in this abandoned house ever since."

"What a sad story," said Elmo sympathetically. "But you should have come to town and made friends. We're very nice folks."

"I was afraid you wouldn't like a witch's cat," said Sheba. "Besides, I knew nothing could be done until Halloween came again. That's the only time witches have flying privileges."

"So why did you steal everyone's jack-o'-lanterns?" asked Detective Mole.

Sheba answered, "I only borrowed them. I planned to light them all as a signal that even my mistress could see when she comes flying over town at midnight on her way to the Witches' Council. I planned to return the jack-o'-lanterns with a thank-you note as soon as she found me."

"What a terrific plan!" Detective Mole exclaimed. "Let us help you. Wait here until Elmo and I return."

Detective Mole and Elmo ran to town and told everyone about Sheba.

"Come and help us get Sheba back to her mistress," they said. "We'll have a party. And what better place is there to celebrate Halloween than at the old, abandoned house?"

Everyone liked the idea of a party. They were all feeling in the spirit of Halloween again, now that their jack-o'-lanterns had been found.

"HURRAY!" they all shouted.

The whole town came to the party. Everyone wanted to meet Sheba, the guest of honor, and was excited about the chance of seeing a real live witch. They all arrived in costume, and raced around the house scaring one another and stuffing themselves with Halloween candy, cookies, and punch.

Just before midnight, Detective Mole got everyone together and had them light their jack-o'-lanterns and take them outside. Then he showed them where to place them on the ground. The lighted jack-o'-lanterns spelled out the words: SHEBA IS HERE!

Everyone stood very quietly and looked upward. Exactly at midnight they spotted something sweeping across the sky.

"Look!" cried Elmo. "It's the witch! And she sees our signal."

Sure enough, the witch came swooping down on her broom. Sheba leaped up just as the broom touched the ground. The witch grabbed her in her arms and hugged her close. Everyone laughed and cried at the happy reunion.

Sheba turned to Detective Mole. "How can I ever thank you," she said.

"Think nothing of it," said Detective Mole. "It was all in a day's work. Here, have a jellybean."

Sheba popped a black jellybean into her mouth. Then she hopped on the broom and she and her mistress flew away. And the last anyone heard was Sheba calling:

"HAPPY HALLOWEEN, EVERYONE!
I'LL SEE YOU NEXT YEAR!"

So ended another case for Detective Mole.

About the Author

Robert Quackenbush is a prolific children's book author and illustrator who lives in New York City with his wife and son, Piet.